SO, YOU WANT TO BE AN ATHLETE?

SO, YOU WANT TO BE AN ATHLETE?

BRANDIN BRYANT

THIS BOOK BELONGS TO

_____

_____

_____

PALMETTO
PUBLISHING
Charleston, SC
www.PalmettoPublishing.com

Copyright © 2023 by Brandin's Books LLC

All rights reserved
No portion of this book may be reproduced, stored in a retrieval system, or transmitted in any form by any means–electronic, mechanical, photocopy, recording, or other–except for brief quotations in printed reviews, without prior permission of the author.

First Edition

Paperback ISBN: 979-8-8229-2413-0
Hardcover ISBN: 979-8-8229-4075-8

THIS BOOK IS DEDICATED
TO ALL THE
FUTURE SUPERSTARS!

So, you want to be an athlete
and play all types of sports?
Let's talk about what it takes
to make it on the field and on the court.

So, you want to be an athlete?
I'm sure you could.
But first, you better make sure
that your grades are really good.

FIRST, YOU MUST PRACTICE,
LIFT WEIGHTS, AND STRETCH.
BUT IF YOU DON'T DO WELL IN SCHOOL,
THIS DREAM IS FAR-FETCHED.

MANY HAVE THIS DREAM,
BUT MANY DO NOT LAST.
YOU LOVE SPORTS SO MUCH,
AND YOU BELIEVE YOU'RE UP TO THE TASK.

MANY CAN THROW,
AND MANY CAN PASS.
BUT MANY BOYS AND GIRLS
DO NOT DO WELL IN CLASS.

THIS JOURNEY IS LONG,
SO YOU MUST GET A GRIP!
DID I FORGET TO MENTION?
YOU NEED GOOD GRADES TO EARN A SCHOLARSHIP!

THROUGHOUT THE YEARS,
MANY CAME, AND MANY WENT.
MUCH TIME AND MANY DOLLARS
HAVE BEEN FOOLISHLY SPENT.

OPPORTUNITIES HAVE BEEN WASTED
BECAUSE SOME DO NOT WORK
AND INSTEAD CHOOSE TO REST.
TALENT HAS BEEN WASTED
BECAUSE SOME DO NOT
GIVE IT THEIR BEST.

NO TIME FOR LAZINESS
ON THIS FIELD OF GLAMOUR AND GLEAM.
IF YOU WANT TO PLAY THIS GAME,
YOU MUST DO MORE THAN DREAM.

IF YOU WANT TO BE AN ATHLETE,
JUST ASK ME!
HARD WORK BEATS TALENT EVERY TIME,
SOON YOU WILL SEE!

MANY CAN THROW, MANY CAN TACKLE,
AND MANY CAN PASS.
BUT TO SOME, A DREAM IS ONLY A DREAM,
AND A DREAM WITHOUT DEDICATION WILL NEVER LAST.

SO, IF YOU WANT TO PLAY SPORTS,
MAKE UP YOUR MIND.
IF YOU STRADDLE THE FENCE,
YOU ARE WASTING YOUR TIME.

A LONG JOURNEY AWAITS, AND AT FIRST,
YOU MAY NOT WIN.
TO ACHIEVE THIS DREAM, YOU MUST TRY AND TRY,
AND THEN TRY AGAIN.

EVERY ATHLETE STARTS AS A KID
WITH A VISION AND A DREAM,
TO PLAY UNDER THE LIGHTS,
AND IN FRONT OF MANY ON THE BIG TV SCREEN!

NO FEELING IN THE WORLD IS BETTER
THAN YOUR CLEATS ON THE GREEN,
OR DOING WHAT YOU LOVE
AND CELEBRATING WITH YOUR TEAM.

SOME ARE LAZY. SOME WORK HARD.
AND SOME ARE IN BETWEEN.
ONLY THE HARDEST WORKERS MAKE IT FAR,
FROM WHAT I HAVE SEEN.

BUT MANY WILL TRY
AND FALL SHORT.
THEY SAY THEY DON'T KNOW WHY,
THAT THEY LOVE THIS SPORT.

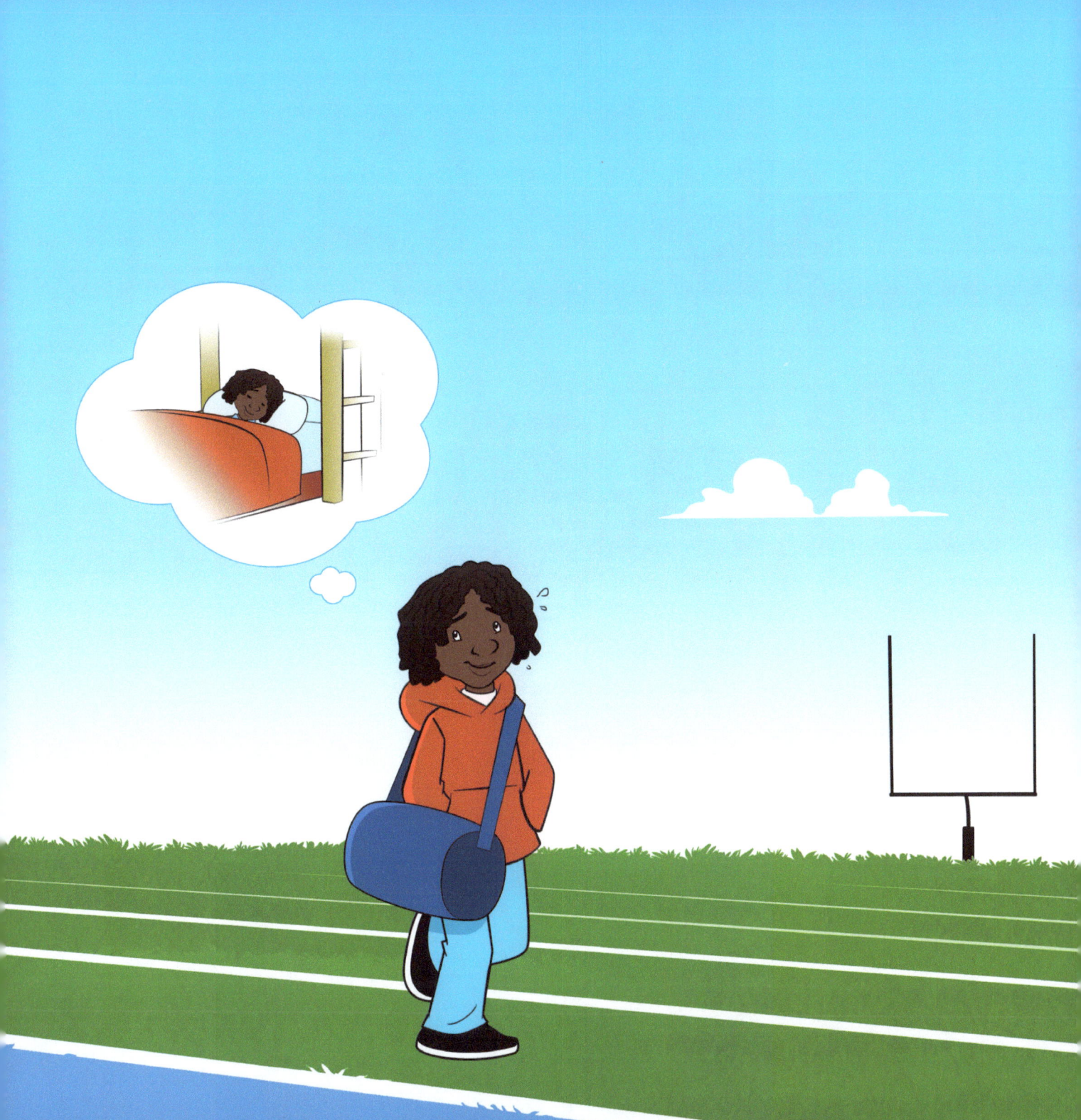

IF YOU WANT TO BE THE BEST.
YOU MUST MEAN IT!
BECAUSE MANY HAVE SUCCEEDED.
I HAVE SEEN IT!

THOSE WHO HAVE MADE IT TRAINED
HARDER THAN THE REST.
THOSE WHO HAVE MADE IT
DID WELL ON THEIR TESTS.

TRAIN DAILY, PRACTICE MATH,
AND PICK UP A BOOK ON A SHELF.
I KNOW WHAT IT TAKES
BECAUSE I HAVE MADE IT MYSELF.

THE ONES WHO MADE IT LOVED THE GAME,
BUT THEY ALSO LOVED SCHOOL.
NOT ONLY DID THEY HAVE A DREAM,
BUT THEY KNEW THAT GOOD GRADES WERE COOL!

Brandin Bryant is a professional football player in the NFL (National Football League). He is a mental performance enthusiast and a first-time author.

Brandin is originally from Omaha, Nebraska. He believes that a growth mindset is imperative. Brandin has been invited to speak at many universities across the nation to share his story, experiences, and outlooks on what it takes to succeed in the realm of professional and amateur athletics. Brandin, an undrafted free agent out of Florida Atlantic University, has played eight years (and counting) of professional football.

Brandin currently resides in Boca Raton, FL.

 @BRANDINSBOOKS

 WWW.BRANDINSBOOKS.COM

IF YOU ENJOYED THIS BOOK,
PLEASE TAKE A FEW MOMENTS
TO WRITE A REVIEW ON
YOUR SELECTED RETAILER'S WEBSITE!

THANK YOU!

www.ingramcontent.com/pod-product-compliance
Lightning Source LLC
LaVergne TN
LVHW070442070526
838199LV00036B/682